To Cuspadora, a.k.a. my mother, Shelly Marshall.

Love you—Karmal Korn.

—K. W.

For Levi

XXX

—J. C.

MARGARET K. McELDERRY BOOKS

An imprint of Simon & Schuster Children's Publishing Division

1230 Avenue of the Americas, New York, New York 10020

Text copyright © 2011 by Karma Wilson

Illustrations copyright © 2011 by Jane Chapman

All rights reserved, including the right of reproduction in whole or in part in any form.

MARGARET K. McELDERRY BOOKS is a trademark of Simon & Schuster, Inc.

Book edited by Emma D. Dryden

Book designed by Lauren Rille

The text for this book is set in Adobe Caslon.

The illustrations for this book are rendered in acrylic paint.

ISBN 978-1-4169-5855-0

Printed at RR Donnelley, Reynosa,

Tamaulipas, Mexico

July 2011

Bear's Loose Tooth

Karma Wilson

illustrations by Jane Chapman

Margaret K. McElderry Books

New York   London   Toronto   Sydney

To Michaela,
Happy 4th Birthday
Sweet Girl —
We love you so much!
Andi + Shirley

From a cave in the forest
came a MUNCH, MUNCH, CRUNCH
as Bear and his friends
all nibbled on their lunch.

Bear savored every bite.
He gulped and he gobbled.
Then there in his mouth
something wiggled, and it wobbled.

As Bear nibbled food,
something moved when he chewed!
It was ...
Bear's
loose
tooth!

Bear pointed in his mouth
and he said, "Oh, dear!
My tooth feels funny.
It's the one right here."

Bear frowned and he worried.
Tears welled in his eyes.
"But how will I eat
if my tooth says good-bye?"

Hare said, "Open wide."
Then he looked inside
and saw
Bear's
loose
tooth.

Mouse squeaked, "Don't fret.
Don't fuss. Look, see?
A new tooth will grow
where the old used to be."

"We'll help!" said Wren.
"I know what to do!
It's out with the old
and in with the new!"

Wren perched on Bear's lip
and he got a good grip
on
Bear's
loose
tooth.

Wren pulled on the tooth
with all of his might.
"Is it out?" asked Bear.
But it stayed stuck tight.

"I'm a bit too small
for the job," said Wren.
So Owl grabbed the tooth.
But the tooth stayed in.

Badger said, "I'll try."
And he gave a big pry
on
Bear's
loose
tooth.

They all took a turn,
but the tooth wouldn't budge.

Then . . .

Bear used his tongue
and he gave a little nudge.
His tooth wiggled to and fro;
then what do you know . . .

Bear's
tooth
fell
OUT!

Bear danced a big dance.
Bear grinned a big grin.
Bear held up his tooth
and he showed all his friends.

Bear looked in the mirror,
and he laughed at his smile.
A new tooth *would* come,
but it might take a while.

That night in bed, right next to his head
lay
Bear's
loose
tooth.

While he slept and he snored,
a fairy fluttered in,
and she left blueberries
where Bear's tooth had been!

He woke in the morning
and found the sweet treat.
Bear's friends came for breakfast.
They sat down to eat.

Bear gulped and he gobbled,
and he felt something wobble. . . .

Uh-oh!

Bear's
loose
tooth!